ALL MY OWN WORK

Adventures in Art

carole Armstrong and Anthea Peppin

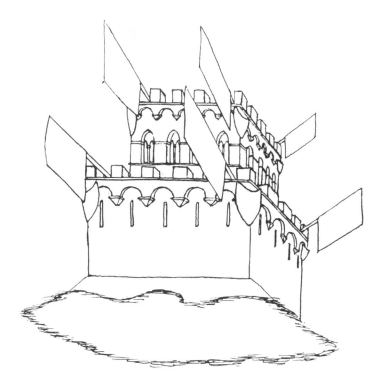

FRANCES LINCOLN CHILDREN'S BOOKS
in association with National Gallery Publications, London

D0183782

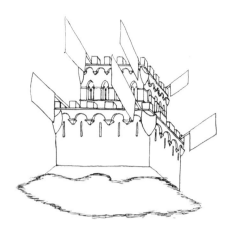

First published in Great Britain in 1993 by Frances Lincoln Children's Books,
4 Torriano Mews, Torriano Avenue, London NW5 2RZ
www.franceslincoln.com

This paperback edition published in 2005

Distributed in the USA by Publishers Group West

British Library Cataloguing in Publication Data available on request

ISBN 1-84507-353-3

Printed in China
9 8 7 6 5 4 3 2 1

All my own Work!

ADVENTURES IN ART

What's an adventure in art?

It might be anything: a dragon to fight, a ride on a magic castle, a mystery ship sailing in to shore, an empty frame to fill with all your own work… An adventure is whatever you make it, with the help of paints, crayons, pencils, felt-tips, scraps of paper, scissors, glue, and anything else you can think of – but above all, imagination!

There is a new adventure on each double page. Some have two or three parts – if so, the simplest parts come first. You can tackle the adventures in any order, but the easiest ones are near the front of the book. Every double page has a note that gives some ideas or practical hints – you can read them or not, as you choose!

The starting point for each adventure is an image from a painting in the National Gallery, London. You can see the complete painting if you go to the gallery, and you can find a small picture of each one used in this book inside the back cover.

Ready? Turn the page, and have fun!

MIRROR, MIRROR!

Your penfriend wants to know exactly what you look like, but you can't send a photograph: you've no camera.

● Draw a big, close-up portrait of yourself inside the frame, to show your penfriend what you look like. Don't forget to show your arm joined on to the hand resting on the edge of the frame!

● Write your name and the date underneath your portrait, and write something beneath it: a line of poetry you like, a message in code or something else that you want to send your penfriend.

A self-portrait is just what it sounds like – a portrait the artist does of him or herself. A self-portrait can show as much of the body as you want it to: just the face, just the head and shoulders, the body above the waist, or even more. Sometimes the artist writes a comment beneath the portrait as well as signing it or adding the date.

Murillo: *Self Portrait*

NO PAINTBRUSH!

You've lost your paintbrush, the shops are shut, but you can't wait to start painting. Use your fingers and any other tools you can get hold of – a comb, an old toothbrush, a blunt, bendy knife – and *very* thick paint (see page 48).

● Paint the vase, and use your tools to give it an interesting pattern.

● Fill the vase with flowers: they could be more sunflowers, or any mixture of flowers you like – roses, marigolds, daisies, pansies… Put some leaves or grasses in too, if you want to.

● Use your tools to give your plants and flowers different textures.

Van Gogh, whose painting *Sunflowers* this vase comes from, used oil paint in quite a different way from other painters. He put it very thickly on to the canvas using a large brush, a knife, and maybe even his fingers. The paint is so thick that it forms ridges and troughs. There is an enlargement of part of *Sunflowers*, next to the whole painting, inside the back cover.

Van Gogh: *Sunflowers*

ACTION!

Have you ever wanted to fight a dragon? Here's your chance!

• The dragon hasn't turned up yet. Before it arrives, draw yourself sitting on the horse, complete with a suit of armour and a shiny weapon, ready for battle.

• Create a really terrifying dragon to tackle. Where do you think your dragon would be in the picture?

• You aren't alone…somebody (or something) else is with you. Add them to your picture.

There are different ways to draw or paint an animal so that it looks as if it is moving. If you find Crivelli's picture of *Saint George and the Dragon* inside the back cover, you will see that the horse is rearing up and twisting round as the saint raises his sword behind his head, ready to bring it crashing down on the dragon.

Crivelli: *Saint George and the Dragon*

LIGHT AND DARK

It's winter and a storm is coming…

- Make some clouds from torn-up newspaper and glue them onto the sky. You could add trees, too – just bare, black shapes outlined against the sky or ground.

- A castle gets draughty in winter. Cut out square bits of newspaper and glue them on to the walls to keep out the wind.

- The people who live in the castle have come out to enjoy themselves before the storm. Some of them have animals with them. Use pencil or pen to add their black shapes in front of the castle.

If you look inside the back cover for the picture of *The Castle of Muiden in Winter*, you will see that the artist made it look wintry by using lots of different greys and hardly any bright colours. He made the trees and people very dark so that they stand out against the lighter background. They are almost in silhouette, like the small figures around this page.

Beerstraaten: *The Castle of Muiden in Winter*

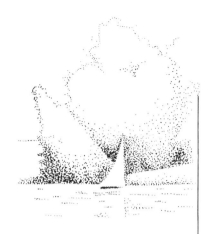

DOTS AND BLOBS

You have thought up a brilliant new way to paint! Instead of mixing colours in your paint box, why not put dots of different colours side by side on your painting?

● Try out your brainwave with felt-tip pens around the frame on the opposite page.

● The picture inside the frame looks empty. What else might it show? Finish the picture off with dots and blobs, big and bold. (Use two felt-tips held together for speed.)

Strangely enough, other artists have had the same idea as you! Look inside the back cover for the picture by Seurat called *Bathers at Asnières*, and the enlargement of one section that shows how it was painted. Rather than mixing the colours together on his palette, Seurat wanted the colours to mix in your eye when you look at the picture from far away. He sometimes framed his pictures with dots too.

Seurat: *Bathers at Asnières*

AN EYE FOR DETAIL

Your cat went missing. You spent all morning hunting for him high and low. Now, at last, you have found him, just in time to save him from…what?

● Fill in as many details as you can to show where your cat is.

● Add whatever he is watching to your picture.

● Lots of other cats have turned up to watch. Put them in too: large ones, small ones, black, white, tabby, ginger… Make them look as real as you can.

Van Mieris, who painted the picture the little cat comes from, painted in great detail. He used the finest brushes and worked so carefully that you can't see the brush-strokes on his paintings at all. Some artists who painted fine detail may have used a magnifying glass to help them see what they were doing more clearly.

Van Mieris: *A Woman and a Fish-pedlar*

FRAMED!

You were secretly following someone when they disappeared though this splendid archway. You aren't sure what's on the other side, so you tiptoe up the step and peer through.

● Draw or paint what you can see through the archway.

● Looking down, you see three things on the step. The person you were following must have dropped them! Add them to your picture.

● Suddenly something makes you look up…what do you see above the archway?

How many pictures can you find inside the back cover that show people or places seen through some sort of frame: a window, a doorway, an arch, or a view through trees and bushes?

In the picture by Crivelli on page 48 the Virgin Mary is framed in a doorway. (If you look hard you can see the objects the artist painted on the step at the front.)

Antonello da Messina: *Saint Jerome in his Study*

FOUR SEASONS

Your crystal ball lets you see the same place at different times of year. Look into it now.

● Write the name of a different season underneath each circle, and then make the tree look as it would at that time of year. (Don't fill up the whole circle yet!)

● Look into your crystal ball again and then fill in the rest of the scene for each season. What is the weather like? If there are people or animals, what are they doing?

● Why not draw or paint around the outside of the circles too? You could put in flowers, birds, animals – anything that reminds you of a particular season.

The tree comes from a wintry painting by Avercamp – you can find it inside the back cover. Looking at it is almost like looking through a round window at the busy scene the artist saw.

Artists sometimes use special colour schemes for seasons. Summer might have hot colours like reds, oranges and yellows, while winter might have lots of cool blues, whites and neutral colours.

Avercamp: *A Winter Scene with Skaters near a Castle*

19

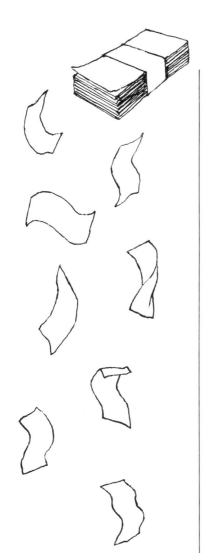

CARICATURE

● The character without a face is a really terrifying person: give him the most frightening face you can.

● There's some money on the table, but it's not enough! Make some coin rubbings on paper, cut them out and stick them in (see page 48).

● There still isn't enough money on the table! Add other kinds of treasure: bars of gold, bank notes, piles of jewels. Stick gold or silver foil on to your treasure hoard, to make it look even more valuable.

A caricature exaggerates some aspect of a person's face or body, sometimes in a nasty way, to criticise their character. The artist who painted this picture, Marinus, was well-known for his caricatures of certain kinds of people, including misers.

If you look on page 48 you'll find another caricature, from a painting by Hogarth. What sort of character do you think it shows?

Marinus van Reymerswaele: *Two Tax Gatherers*

CASTLE IN THE AIR

● This magical castle is floating in the sky. Who does it belong to? Put something on the flags as a clue to who the imaginary owner is.

● You are right at the top of the castle, looking out: what can you see? Clouds, stars, rooftops? What is the weather like?

● Someone has seen you and they are *really* surprised. Where are they? Draw in the onlooker and show what they are feeling.

Sassetta painted this castle as part of a dream. His picture, inside the back cover, shows the castle floating over a little town. Saint Francis is asleep, and the angel is showing him in a dream that one day he will be the leader of a special religious group called the Franciscan Order. The Franciscans use a red cross as their symbol, so the flags are a clue.

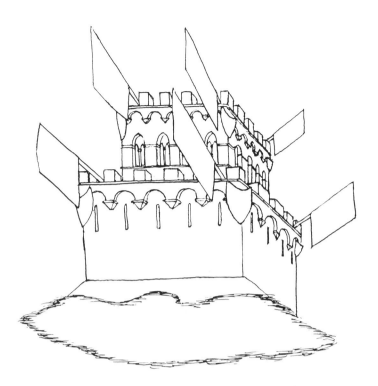

ARTIST AT WORK!

Long ago, an artist began to paint… Here is part of his room, and lots of the bits and pieces he used in his work.

● The artist has run out of shelf space: make the top shelf longer and draw some more strange jars and bottles for him to use.

● The painting on the easel has vanished! Fill it in with whatever you like: a face, a place, a story… You'll need a sharp pencil or crayons, or a pen with a fine tip.

● You are an artist too! Show yourself hard at work painting the painter, with all the bits and pieces *you* use.

When this picture was painted artists had to make their own paints. The colours came from minerals, earths and dyes made from plants or insects. The artists ground the raw materials into powder, then mixed them with something sticky like egg yolk to make paint.

SWIRLS AND WHIRLS

● It's a windy day. Draw or paint other trees tossing about in the wind beside the one that's already here.

● The gale is getting stronger: try sticking bits of torn-up tissue paper on to the picture, or blowing trickles of paint across the page with a straw, to show what is happening to the leaves and flowers.

● There are other things blowing about in the air, in the sky, and on the ground. Add them to your picture!

The tree comes from a picture by Van Gogh. He found a way to suggest movement in his paintings using swirling, curling, wavy lines painted with very thick paint. Other artists show people or animals running or objects swishing about, or paint people wearing clothes that curl up in the wind, like the figure by Titian on page 48.

Van Gogh: *A Wheatfield, with Cypresses*

FILL THE SHELVES

You are almost out of food – time for a trip to the shops.

● Draw or paint what your food shelf looks like after you come home loaded with your favourite fruit and vegetables.

● Fruit and vegetables aren't all you bought! Draw in more shelves and fill them with bottles, tins, packets and jars of every shape and size that you brought home from your shopping trip.

● Packets and tins need labels: make some for the ones on your shelves. (Draw or paint them, or cut up old labels or magazines and glue them in.)

Paintings of flowers, food, pots and pans and other everyday things are called still-life. Many artists like to make you want to reach out and touch the different surfaces and rearrange the shapes. Sometimes they paint tiny insects like beetles, snails and butterflies in among the fruit and flowers. They look almost real!

Meléndez: *Still Life with Oranges and Walnuts*

HOW DO YOU FEEL?

● This is a picture of you and a friend, up to something! What are you both holding?

● Draw in faces on yourself and your friend. Make the faces show how you feel.

● Someone else has sneaked into the picture: who are they and what are they up to? Add whoever you like.

Grown-ups often look very serious in paintings, especially if the painting is a portrait, like the one by Jan van Eyck on page 48. If you look inside the back cover for the picture by Judith Leyster that these children come from, you can see that they don't look serious at all. They weren't having their portraits painted, and they look as if they are having fun.

Leyster: *A Boy and a Girl*

SHADOW PLAY

It's evening and the shadows are lengthening. The watchers on the shore are waiting anxiously for a ship to appear.

● Draw in the shadows of the people on the shore. Can you see the sun? Which way should the shadows be pointing?

● At last, here comes the ship! It's a sailing ship, with a tall mast and billowing sails. Draw or paint it, complete with its shadow.

● Somebody is very happy to see the ship sail in. Draw or paint them somewhere in your picture, showing how glad they are.

Shadows don't always look the same, and they need not be black: coloured light casts coloured shadows. You can often guess what time of day it is in a painting by seeing how long the shadows are.

The seaport here is from a painting by Claude: find it inside the back cover and see what time of day you think it represents.

Claude: *A Seaport*

WHAT'S YOUR VIEW?

You woke up this morning, pulled back the curtain, and saw a city you'd never set eyes on before, with streets full of water, and strange, wonderful buildings.

• Draw in as much as possible of what you can see from your window.

• People travel by boat in this city. Cut out some boats from old magazines and stick them on to your drawing.

Canaletto, the artist who painted this city, was famous for his accurate, detailed views of canals, rivers and street scenes in Venice and London. This style of painting was very popular with English buyers.

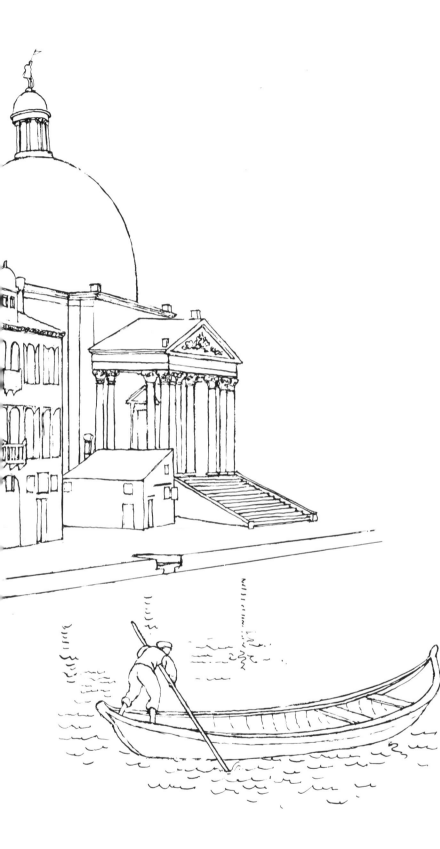

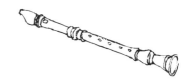

MUSIC MAKERS

It's time for some fun, and the music is about to begin…

• The players have lost their musical instruments: draw them some replacements. (If you can't think of an instrument for them to play, make something up.)

• You aren't just an artist – now you're a musician too! Draw yourself next to the children, with an instrument that *you* would like to play.

• Where is the performance going to happen: on a stage, in a garden, in the street? It might be somewhere far stranger than that. Draw in the surroundings you imagine.

From the earliest paintings in Ancient Greece, China and Rome right up until today, artists have put music and musical instruments into their paintings. Paintings show everyone, from the rich to the poor, playing in concerts, playing for festivals, or just playing for fun. You'll find another picture of music makers on page 48.

Molenaer: *Children making Music*

UPSIDE-DOWN IMAGES

Many artists love to paint reflections, but they can be difficult, and even the greatest artists sometimes get them wrong.

Can you work out what the reflections of the swan and the bridge should look like? Try to draw in the reflections, then turn to page 48 to see if you were right.

It's Halloween!

● Think of some spooky things to add to the sky above the castle.

● The castle is on an island. Draw in the water and an upside-down picture of the castle reflected in it. ·

● A strange procession of people is about to set out towards the castle. They might be swimming, or flying, or they might be in boats. Add them and their reflections to your picture.

Cuyp: *Ubbergen Castle*

TELLING STORIES

Something extraordinary has just happened, and you saw it all! However, you are in a country where nobody speaks your language. All you can do is rush to the nearest newspaper office and draw or paint a picture showing the whole story...

● Finish off the picture on the opposite page to show the newspaper people exactly what happened. (Don't forget to put yourself in it.)

● You hope your story is going to make your fortune. Does it? Draw a cartoon strip across the bottom of this page to show what happens after you show the newspaper people your story.

Sassetta painted lots of stories about Saint Francis. This one is about how he persuaded a ferocious wolf to stop eating the people who lived in the town of Gubbio in Italy, in return for the people giving the wolf other food instead.

Sassetta: *The Legend of the Wolf of Gubbio*

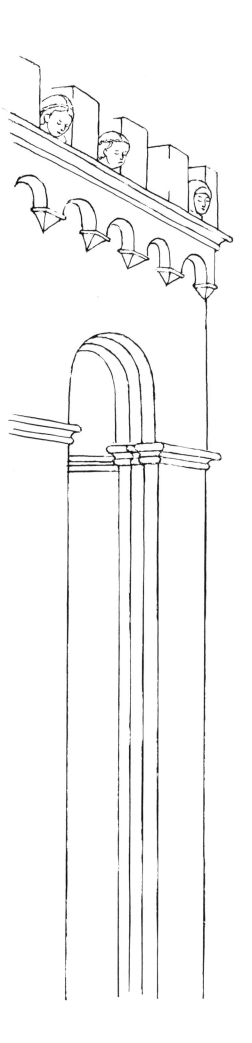

WHOSE THRONE?

You are a designer with a strange new customer called Night. Night has seen this magnificent throne you made for Neptune, King of the Sea. Now Night wants a special throne too.

● Draw or sketch a special throne for Night. Try to make it show the animals, birds and things that make you think of night time.

● Use gold and silver foil or shiny sweet wrappers to make the throne look as splendid as you can.

● What does your strange customer look like? Draw or paint Night standing beside the magnificent new throne.

Do the small pictures on this page make you think of anything, like Peace or Time or Love? When an object is used to stand for an idea, it is called a symbol. Guessing what the symbols in a picture mean helps you understand more about it.

Tura: *An Allegorical Figure*

BATTLEGROUND!

There's a battle going on – or is it just a tournament? You're there, so you decide!

• Decorate one of the knights to make him stand out. You could use paints or crayons, or stick on pieces of tin foil or coloured paper.

• Add some people in the distance, fighting, or watching, or running away. Should they be bigger than the knights or smaller?

More than 500 years ago, artists became interested in making pictures look as like the real world as possible. They noticed that things close to us seem large, while things that are far away appear to be small. The picture by Hobbema on page 48 shows very clearly how this works.

Uccello: *Niccolò Mauruzi da Tolentino at the Battle of San Romano*

SUNLIGHT

It's a scorching hot day on the beach. The sun is dazzling. The sand and the sky and the water are blindingly bright.

● To get the effect of sunlight, dab a little water on to the paper where the sky and sand should be – just enough to make the paper damp.

● Using your paints, mix a pale colour for the sky and dab it on with a very small sponge. Then mix another pale colour and do the same for the sand.

● You are on the beach somewhere. Add yourself to the picture doing whatever you like doing on a hot day at the beach.

Until about a hundred years ago, artists almost always painted indoors. Then, when paints could be bought ready-made in tubes that were easy to carry about, artists found that it was quite easy to paint in the open air.

Monet, whose picture this woman comes from, painted it on the beach: some grains of sand have been found in the paint!

Monet: *The Beach at Trouville*

Thick paint page 6
Try using thick poster paints (use straight from the pot), or powder paints (with a very small amount of water), or ready-made finger paints (you can buy these from toy shops, art suppliers and some stationery shops).

Coin rubbing page 20
You will need some coins, thin white tracing or typing paper, and a pencil with dark lead or a black wax crayon.

Place a coin under the paper. Hold it down firmly with one hand while you carefully rub across the top of the paper with your pencil or crayon. Like magic, the shape of your coin will appear! You can cut out the rubbings and glue them on to your drawing.

Upside-down images page 38

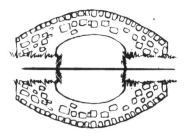

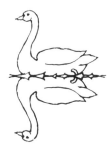

Carlo CRIVELLI (active 1457-94(?))
The Annunciation, with Saint Emidius

TITIAN (active before 1511; died 1576)
Bacchus and Ariadne (detail)

Lorenzo COSTA (1459/60-1535)
A Concert

Jan van EYCK (active 1422; died 1441)
A Man in a Turban

Meyndert HOBBEMA (1638-1709)
The Avenue, Middelharnis

William HOGARTH (1697-1764)
Marriage à la Mode: The Visit to the Quack Doctor (detail)